Top Puppies – **Rourke**

8 Volumes

List Price $ $27.07 **/ Our Price $ $18.95**
Set Price $ $151.60

ISBN	Title
978-173162-8732	Boxer Puppies
978-173162-8626	Bulldog Puppies
978-173162-8701	German Shepherd Puppies
978-173162-8558	Golden Retriever Puppies
978-173162-8596	Labrador Retriever Puppies
978-173162-8657	Poodle Puppies
978-173162-8763	Pug Puppies
978-173162-8688	Yorkshire Terrier Puppies

P.O. Box 3005 | Mankato, MN 56002
(800) 783-6767 (P) | (412) 688-8545 (F)
customerservice@applebks.com
www.applebks.com

Table of Contents

Labrador Retriever Puppies   3

Photo Glossary   15

Index   16

About the Author   16

Rourke
Educational Media

A Division of
Carson Dellosa Education

rourkeeducationalmedia.com

Can you find these words?

ball

fur

puppies

run

Labrador Retriever Puppies

puppies

These are Labrador Retriever **puppies!**
They are called Labs.

What do Lab puppies look like?

4

They have thick **fur**.

They get big. They grow to 23 inches (58 centimeters) tall.

What do Lab puppies act like?

They are full of energy.
They like to **run**.

They can learn games.

They can fetch a **ball.**

ball

They like people.

They love kids!

Did you find these words?

They can fetch a **ball**.

They have thick **fur**.

These are Labrador Retriever **puppies**!

They like to **run**.

Photo Glossary

 **ball** (bawl): A round object that is used for games.

 **fur** (fur): The coat of hair on the skin of an animal.

 **puppies** (PUHP-eez): Dogs that are young and not fully grown.

 **run** (ruhn): To move faster than a walk.

Index

big 6

energy 9

fetch 11

games 10

kids 13

people 12

About the Author

Hailey Scragg is a writer from Ohio. She loves all puppies, especially her puppy, Abe! She likes taking him on long walks in the park.

PHOTO CREDITS: cover: ©cmannphoto, ©manley099 (bone); back cover: ©ilona75 (inset), ©Naddiya (pattern); pages 2, 3, 14, 15: ©chris-mueller; pages 2, 4-5, 14, 15: ©Vera Larina; page 6: ©Bigandt_Photography; page 7: ©MagnusPersson; page 2, 8-9, 14, 15: ©Ridofranz; pages 2, 10-11, 14, 15: ©areacreative; pages 12-13: ©hartcreations

Edited by: Kim Thompson
Cover and interior design by: Janine Fisher

Library of Congress PCN Data
Labrador Retriever Puppies / Hailey Scragg
(Top Puppies)
ISBN 978-1-73162-859-6 (hard cover)(alk. paper)
ISBN 978-1-73162-858-9 (soft cover)
ISBN 978-1-73162-860-2 (e-Book)
ISBN 978-1-73163-340-8 (ePub)
Library of Congress Control Number: 2019945512

Printed in the United States of America,
North Mankato, Minnesota